Collect all the No. 1 Boy Detective books!

NO.1 BOY DETECTIVE

Dog
Snatchers

NO.1 BOY DETECTIVE

Dog Snatchers

Barbara Mitchelhill
Illustrated by
Tony Ross

Andersen Press • London

For Katy Lily with love

This edition first published in 2017 by
Andersen Press Limited
20 Vauxhall Bridge Road
London SW1V 2SA
www.andersenpress.co.uk

First published by Andersen Press Limited in 2008

2 4 6 8 10 9 7 5 3 1

British Library Cataloguing in Publication Data available.

ISBN 978 1 78344 667 4

Printed and bound in Turkey by Omur Printing Co, Istanbul

Chapter 1

I expect you know my name. Damian Drooth Supersleuth and Ace Detective. People come from miles around to ask for my help. But let me tell you about a crime I solved only last week. It wasn't easy. It took all my brain power and cunning to crack this one.

It was Saturday morning and the gang was in the shed. I was explaining how to spot criminal disguises such as wigs and dark glasses.

'My gwandad's got a wig,' said Lavender. ''Coth he hathn't got any hair.'

'Your grandad could be telling porky pies,' I said. 'He's probably got loads of hair. I bet he's really a criminal who doesn't want to be spotted by the police. That's why he wears a wig.' Lavender started crying. I wasn't surprised. It's hard to learn the truth – especially when you're only six.

I carried on in spite of the noise. But before I got to the really interesting bit about wearing hats and old clothes, there was a knock on the shed door. Everyone – even Lavender – went quiet and I went to see who it was.

When I opened the door, I found an

old lady standing there. She was small with white curly hair.

'Excuse me,' she said. 'Are you Damian Drooth?'

'Who's asking?' I said, not wanting to give anything away.

'I'm Mrs Popperwell,' she said.

I was suspicious. I'd never heard that name before . . . Popperwell . . . It was probably false – and her hair looked like a wig to me. I would have to be on my guard.

'Why are you looking for Damian Drooth?' I asked.

She took a tissue from her handbag. 'Because Blossom has gone missing,' she said, wiping away tears (which might have been false).

'Missing?' I said.

'For two hours.'

'That's not so long.'

'My Blossom never goes out,' she sobbed. 'Not without me.'

'That's strange,' I said. 'Most girls like to play with their friends.'

'She's not a girl. She's a dog and I'm ever so worried.'

'So why didn't you go to the police?'

'Because I've heard that Damian Drooth is a brilliant detective,' she said. 'Only last week I was told that he'd solved a crime at his own school. They say he's better than the police. Much

4

better!'

This was clearly somebody who appreciated me. I took off my baseball cap and my shades to reveal my face.

'I am Damian Drooth,' I said.

Her eyes opened wide in surprise. I could tell she was dead impressed.

'Sorry about all the questions, Mrs Popperwell, but you can't be too careful in the detective business.'

I invited her to come inside and I found a box for her to sit on.

'Now,' I said. 'You'd better tell me all about this Blossom and when she went missing.'

It turned out that Mrs Popperwell had let her dog out in her garden that morning.

'When I called Blossom to come back in – she wasn't there. She had disappeared.' Mrs Popperwell gave her nose a good blow. I think she was pretty upset.

I crunched on some crisps while I thought about the problem.

'It sounds to me,' I said, 'as if we've got Dog Snatchers in the area.'

Mrs Popperwell went as white as a sheet. 'Dog Snatchers?' she gasped. 'What are they?'

'They're people who go around

kidnapping dogs,' I explained. 'In fact, you'll probably get a letter soon demanding a large sum of money.'

She obviously didn't know about such things. I thought she was going to faint.

I offered her a crisp to calm her down. 'Don't worry, Mrs Popperwell,' I said. 'I'll put my detectives on the case. They'll track the criminals down in no time.'

Chapter 2

Winston lived in Richmond Road just round the corner from Mrs Popperwell and her dog.

'I've seen Blossom a few times. She's a poodle with white curly hair and looks quite like Mrs Popperwell.'

'That information could be useful,' I said, noting it in my detective's notebook.

'But I have a plan.'

'Already?' said Tod.

'You're bwilliant, Damian,' said Lavender, who had stopped crying by then. 'You're going to thave Mrs

Popperwell'th doggie becauthe you have the best bwain in all the world.'

I liked Lavender. Nice kid.

'My plan is this,' I said to the gang. 'We make posters and stick them on lampposts and shop windows around the town. A hundred should be enough.'

Everybody thought it was a good scheme.

'How do we get the posters, Damian?'

'We'll make one and then we'll copy it on Mum's photocopier. It shouldn't take long.'

In fact, it took us ages to make the poster. At least ten minutes. I did the writing 'cos mine is the best and the neatest. Winston did the drawing 'cos he knew what Blossom looked like. We put Mrs Popperwell's phone number at the bottom. That was so we could go round to her house and wait for witnesses* to ring.

This was the poster:

This DOG has been stolen
by dangerous
dog Snatchers

Have you seen
anything Suspicious?
phone: 553812 BIG REWARD

Once the poster was finished, I ran up the garden and into the house. Mum

---

* Witness is a word detectives use. It means somebody who saw something. In this case, somebody who saw the Dog Snatchers in action.

was upstairs cleaning the bathroom. She likes doing that kind of thing. It gives her something to do in her spare time.

I didn't want to disturb her so I didn't ask if I could use the photocopier. I knew she wouldn't mind as it was for a good cause. I went into the dining room, switched the machine on and slipped the poster under the lid. I needed a hundred copies, so I tapped in the number.

It was quite an old machine. If you're not careful it flings the copies out and you have to catch them. It's also dead noisy.

That day, Mum must have heard the whirring noise.

'Damian!' she said as she came bursting into the dining room. 'I've told you before about using that photocopier!'

I was taken by surprise and, as I turned round, the copies starting flying off the machine like leaves off a tree.

'It's for a good cause,' I explained as they landed on the carpet. 'A little poodle's gone missing. I'm saving it from Dog Snatchers.'

Any kind-hearted person would have understood. They would have felt sorry for the poor animal. But Mum was not in a good mood.

'The police deal with lost dogs,' she said. 'Now switch that photocopier off at once.'

I tried to explain about how upset Mrs Popperwell was but Mum wouldn't listen. She was in a real temper. She just marched over to the photocopier and pulled the plug out of the socket.

'I've told you not to use it, Damian. Don't waste my paper for one of your detective games! Now go out and play with your friends.'

Did I hear right? Did she think this was all a game? Did she think we were just playing like little kids? I tried to please her by picking up the posters but she went berserk.

'GO!' she shouted. 'NOW!'

So I had to leave without them.

But I didn't give up on my plan.

Chapter 3

'Didn't you manage to get a single poster?' Winston asked.

I shook my head. 'It was a difficult situation. Mum was in one of her moods. I had to get out fast.'

'So what do we do now?'

'We'll write out a hundred posters between us.'

There was a loud groan. I could tell they weren't used to hard work.

'Look!' I said. 'That's only twenty-five each. It won't take long.'

Tod Browning, who is quite good at maths, insisted I'd got it wrong. 'There are five

of us. That means twenty each.'

He didn't understand how to run a crime operation like this. 'Somebody has to be in charge,' I explained.

'Like who?'

'Well, it will have to be me, 'cos I'm the only fully-trained detective.'

I won't bother to tell you what happened next but in the end when the fuss and the arguments had died down, I agreed to help them out – for the sake of solving the crime.

'We'll need five pencils,' said Harry, 'and a hundred sheets of paper.'

'We've all got pencilth,' said Lavender, 'and we could yooth our detective notebookth.'

'Your detective notebooks are no good,' I said. 'We need big sheets of plain paper for posters.'

It was a problem. Mum had already banned me from the house, so I couldn't have her typing paper, but Harry came up with an idea.

'My dad's got something we could use.'

'What?'

'Loads of posters arrived yesterday. He was moaning about them. They're something to do with the council – so they're not important. I think he'll be glad to get rid of them.'

'What's your point, Harry?' I asked.

'Well, they're only printed on one side. We could use the back, see?'

This was just what we needed so I sent Harry to fetch them. Ten minutes later, he was back, staggering under the weight of a box stuffed full of posters.

They were very boring. I could see why his dad didn't want them. They had a photo of a weird-looking woman with frizzy hair, and underneath it said 'Vote for Peacock'. Who would be interested in that? Nobody, that's who. Finding Blossom was a lot

more important.

We turned the posters over and started writing on the blank side.

We wrote: 'This dog has been stolen by dangerous Dog Snatchers' and then did a drawing of Blossom, like before. But writing a lot of posters proved mega difficult. Our hands began to ache and it was dead difficult to do our best writing.

'My fingers are hurting,' said Winston.

'I've got cramp,' said Tod.

'Me, too,' said Lavender.

In the end, we kept it simple.

We did four each, except Lavender who did seven.

We left for the town centre – dumping the unused Peacock posters in a bin. A few blew away but it couldn't be helped.

We stuck our missing dog posters on every lamppost down the High Street and on the newsagent's window as well. I'd got a tube of very strong superglue so they all stuck really well.

The man from the newsagent's didn't seem to like it. He came leaping out of his shop shouting, 'What do you think you're doing?'

We didn't hang around. I knew he'd understand when he read the poster. He might even be able to give us some information.

After that, we went straight round to see Mrs Popperwell to tell her how we were dealing with her case. She was very interested to hear what we had done.

'Posters! That's a marvellous idea,' she said. 'How kind of you.'

We sat by the phone and waited for people to ring with sightings of

Blossom and her kidnappers. In the meantime, Mrs Popperwell brought us cakes and biscuits just to keep our strength up.

But after one packet of HobNobs, several jam tarts and one packet of chocolate cookies, there hadn't been a single call. This was bad. Very bad. How could we solve the crime without some help from the public? Action was needed.

Chapter 4

The idea I came up with could only be described as brilliant.

'We'll use a decoy,' I said.

They didn't understand. 'What's one of them?' Harry asked.

So I explained.

'We let a dog loose down Richmond Road near Mrs Popperwell's house.'

'Why?'

''Cos that's where the Dog Snatchers are operating. We'll wait for them to swoop and take the decoy dog.'

'Then we thend for the powithe,' said Lavender.

'Yes. We send for the police.' She understood. Bright girl, Lavender. She'll make a great detective one day.

'But how do we get a decoy dog?' Harry asked.

'You can use Thumper,' said
Winston. 'He'll trot up and down the
road just as long as there are no cats to
chase.'

'Sorry, but we can't use Thumper.'

'Why?'

'Think about it, Winston. Thumper
wouldn't attract a Dog Snatcher, would
he? He's dirty and scruffy and he smells.
Who would want to steal him?'

Winston went quiet for a bit but I
think he understood.

I chose Curly – Tod and Lavender's
dog – to be our decoy. She wouldn't
exactly win a Top Dog Competition,

but she
was the
best we
had.
 Tod
went to
fetch Curly
while Mrs Popperwell made us a few
sandwiches. By the time Tod came back
with the dog on the lead, we had finished
them. Delicious!

'Thanks, Mrs Popperwell,' I said as
we got up. 'Keep in touch. Let us know
if you get any phone calls or any letters
demanding money.'

'I will,' said Mrs Popperwell as she
waved us off down Richmond Road.

The gang gathered round me on the
pavement. 'What's the plan, Damian?'
they asked.

'First, release Curly,' I said. 'Then spread

out down the road. Keep your eyes on her but stay hidden.'

'How do we do that?'

'There are plenty of bushes around here. Use your detective skills and crouch down behind them so the Dog Snatchers won't see you.'

This was really exciting. Tod unclipped the lead, Curly trotted off and we hid in the gardens, watching from behind the hedges. She was a fantastic decoy dog. She paused every now and then to smell the lampposts. Sometimes, she followed people down

the road – especially those with bags of shopping. And once she got very friendly with an old lady and had a great time with her umbrella. We could see everything from our hide-outs. But just when things were going brilliantly, people spotted us in their gardens and started to get nasty and threw us out.

'You're ruining my plants!' they said.

'Don't climb on that trellis.'

'Get out and stay out.'

I tried explaining that we were working under cover, but it was no good. We were turned out onto the pavement in full view of everyone,

including any passing Dog Snatchers. It's a tough life being a detective.

Just as I was wondering where we could hide, things suddenly began to happen. A man wearing a cap and a large overcoat (could this be a disguise?) came down the road and he called to Curly.

'Here, dog! Good girl! Come and see what I've got.' He had a biscuit in his hand to tempt her.

I alerted the gang at once. Curly, who is a very friendly dog, went right up to the man who immediately pulled the belt off his coat and attached it onto Curly's collar.

'That's him!' I said. 'He's a Dog Snatcher.'

Lavender burst into tears. 'He'th got my doggie! He'th got my doggie!'

I had to get Tod to keep her quiet. I didn't want her giving the game away.

'What do we do now, Damian?' asked Harry.

'You go back to Mrs Popperwell's. Ring the police while we follow the Dog Snatcher.'

'But how can I tell them where to

look for him? You don't know where he'll go.'

Harry was right.

'Forget it,' I said. 'We'll all follow him and see what happens. We don't need the help of the police, do we?'

Chapter 5

We were well on the trail of the Dog Snatcher. He walked all the way down Richmond Road and my gang of detectives stayed a distance behind him so he wouldn't notice us. Halfway down he crossed over, heading for the High Street.

'Clever,' I said.

'Why's that?' Winston asked.

''Cos he's probably parked his car in the multi-storey. We'll have to stop him before he drives off with Curly. She could be lost for ever.'

Lavender set off howling. 'I'll never thee my doggie again!'

Tod found a sweet in his pocket and this shut her up for the time being.

'We'll have to catch up with him,' I said. 'Even if he realises we're on his trail.'

We all raced down the High Street towards the Dog Snatcher.

By the time he reached the newsagent's we were close behind him. Luckily, he stopped to talk to the owner who was trying to scrape our posters off the window. This gave me my chance.

'Call the police,' I yelled to the shopkeeper and grabbed the belt out of the Dog Snatcher's hand. 'This man has stolen our dog. And it's not the first time he's done this kind of thing. Dial 999.'

I could tell that the Dog Snatcher was shocked at being caught by a bunch of kids. He just stood there, his mouth wide open while Lavender pounded him with her little fists and yelled, 'You howid, howid man. You stole my doggie.'

When Curly realised that she'd been saved, she started barking and jumping up at Tod. She was really pleased to see him. A group of people who were doing their shopping, stopped to see what was causing all the fuss. There was quite a crowd.

But the owner of the newsagent's shop wasn't very helpful. He didn't dial 999. In fact he was quite rude.

'Wasn't it you kids who struck this rubbish on my windows?' he said.

What a cheek! No wonder nobody had telephoned Mrs Popperwell with

information. He had removed most of our posters.

The next thing that happened was really lucky. A policeman spotted the crowd in the High Street and came running. He probably thought there was a bank robbery or something.

I explained as quickly as I could.

'My name is Damian Drooth,' I said, 'and these are my trainee detectives.'

'Damian's famous,' Winston added. 'He's one of Inspector Crockitt's advisors.'

The policeman looked down at us, tapping his chin with his finger.

'Damian Drooth, eh?' said the policeman. 'Well, I'm PC Nobbs and I don't believe Inspector Crockitt has ever mentioned you.'

I must admit I was very surprised. 'Take my word for it,' I said. 'And

believe me when I say
that this man is a
Dog Snatcher. You
should question
him about a
dog called
Blossom.
She's gone
missing.'

PC Nobbs didn't
take much notice. He
just looked at Curly.

'So who does this dog belong to?' he
asked.

'It'th my doggie,' said Lavender.

'And mine,' said Tod. 'This girl's my
sister.'

The Dog Snatcher looked very
nervous – a sure sign of a guilty
conscience.

'I . . . I'm sorry, officer,' he said,

'but I'm on business in the area and I saw this dog wandering up and down the road. It was obviously lost. I was worried that it might get run over. I thought I'd better take it to the police station.'

A likely story! But the policeman (who was very inexperienced) believed him.

'That's all right, sir. Just a mistake, I'm sure.' Then PC Nobbs turned to us and said, 'Run along, kiddies, and remember to keep your dog in the garden another time.'

I couldn't believe it! We had caught the Dog Snatcher in the act of dognapping. We had handed him over to the police. And then the police had let him go. Is that scary or what? No dog was safe now that this terrible criminal was on the loose again.

So what should we do?

Chapter 6

'Every dog in this town is in danger,' I explained to the gang, as we walked away. 'We must protect them until the Dog Snatcher has been put behind bars.'

'He'th a howid man,' sobbed Lavender.

I patted her on the head. 'Yes, he's a horrid man all right. But don't you worry, Lavender, I'll have him arrested by tea time.'

My plan was to look out for any dogs in danger. I would make sure they were off the streets for a few hours, until I had found more proof of the Dog Snatcher's criminal activities. Every member of the gang would go down a different street looking for wandering dogs.

'Can I come wiv you, Damian?' Lavender asked.

She didn't want to go on her own. I didn't mind. She could observe and learn more skills that way.

'What'll we do with all the dogs?' Harry asked.

'We'll take them back to my house. They can go in the shed. They'll be safe there.'

We set off looking for dogs in peril. Luckily, I had my binoculars in my pocket. Now I could make sure I didn't miss a thing.

It wasn't long before I found the first one. It had been abandoned in an open-topped sports car in Longdon Street. I looked around for the owner, to warn him of the danger, but I couldn't see anyone.

'I'll leave a note,' I said to Lavender.

I pulled out my detective's notebook and wrote:

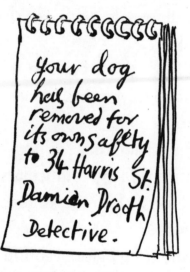

your dog
has been
removed for
its own safety
to 34 Harris St.
Damian Drooth
Detective.

We scooped the dog up and carried it away. Luckily it was only a little black Scottie dog and not too heavy.

And before we reached our street, I spotted another. This time it was a Collie cross tied up to a drainpipe near

the corner shop. If the Dog Snatcher
came along, it would be dead easy to
take him.

'Perhapth the owner'th in the thop,'
said Lavender.

In the shop? Maybe yes. Maybe no.

'Go and thee, Damian.'

Just to please her, I poked my head
inside. There were three people – a man
behind the counter and a man and a
woman buying some dog food.

'Excuse me,' I said. 'I'm Damian

Drooth, detective. Do you realise that the town is on High Alert today?'

They turned round and looked at me as if I was something from outer space. I had probably shocked them. Maybe it was the sight of a black Scottie tucked under my arm. Maybe they had never seen a detective before.

I tried again, speaking more slowly. 'There is a Dog Snatcher on the prowl. I wondered if you knew about it.'

They giggled a bit, then shook their heads.

'No, son,' said the shopkeeper. 'We haven't seen no Dog Snatcher. Not round here, anyway.'

They turned back and carried on putting tins into a carrier bag. It was obvious to my trained eye that they had nothing to do with the Collie cross.

'All systems go, Lavender,' I said

when I came out of the shop. 'They don't know anything.'

Lavender untied the lead from the drainpipe while I wrote another note and stuck it on the wall. Then we set off.

By the time we reached my back garden, there was quite a bit of barking coming from the shed. That was good news. The others must have found loads of dogs out on the streets.

For the time being they were safe but I needed to convince the police that the Dog Snatcher was roaming our town. But how was I going to do that?

Chapter 7

'We're back,' I shouted, as I opened the shed door. It was crammed full of dogs.

Unfortunately, just at that moment, a German shepherd dog bounded out through the gap.

'He's huge,' I said. 'He's the size of

a donkey.'

'I know,' said Harry. 'I found him out in a garden in Trivett Street. He didn't want to come at first but I had a sandwich in my pocket.'

'Smart work, Harry,' I said. 'The owners will be grateful when they learn how you saved him.'

Winston had found two dogs roaming in the park and Tod had

rescued a spaniel from outside the Community Centre.

'They did vewy well,' said Lavender.

'They did,' I said. 'At any minute the Dog Snatcher could have come along and taken them.'

We sat down and had some crisps – all except Winston who decided he had to go home and fetch Thumper.

'I'm worried about him. I left him in our back garden. You never know – he could get snatched.'

Winston left and we finished our crisps.

'What do we do next?' Tod wanted to know. 'We can't keep the dogs here for ever.'

'First things first,' I said. 'They need food and water. I'll go and get some.'

The German shepherd had been having a great time in the garden. As I left the shed, he came running to meet me. Although he was big, he was very friendly. He leapt up and down and then ran in circles flattening Mum's plants, but I didn't think she'd mind. She likes dogs.

He followed me to the back door. 'Stay!' I said and he sat down all right but he started barking. WOOF . . . WOOF . . . WOOF! Big dogs have really loud barks. I just hoped Mum wouldn't hear him.

In the kitchen, I rummaged through the cupboards, found some bowls and filled a bottle with water. There were two tins of stewing steak in the pantry which were perfect for the dogs' dinners. I was just looking in a drawer for the tin opener when the phone rang. I ignored it – Mum would pick it up in the bedroom.

It was not easy, carrying all the doggie things. As I opened the door, the German shepherd burst in, still barking. He bumped right into me and the tins flew out of my hands. So did the dishes, and they smashed on the floor. I tried to calm the dog but he wouldn't stop barking.

Then Mum arrived.

'What on earth's that dog doing in here?'

The German shepherd seemed pleased to see her, too, and jumped up making Mum stagger back a bit until she was pinned against the door.

'Get him off me!' she yelled.

I did my best but it wasn't easy and it

was ages before I managed to push him out into the garden.

Mum was not in a good mood. I have noticed lately that she gets easily upset. Maybe she needs a holiday. Disney World would be good.

'DAMIAN! LISTEN TO ME!' she shouted as if I was as deaf as Grandad. 'Why is this animal in my garden? And why do I keep getting phone calls from people accusing me of taking their

dogs? WHAT'S GOING ON, DAMIAN?'

Luckily, there was a knock at the front door and Mum went to see who it was. It turned out to be PC Nobbs who we'd met outside the newsagent's. Mum brought him into the kitchen to meet me. Apparently a man in the park had seen Winston walk off with his dog and had phoned the police. (A bit sneaky, I thought.)

'I guessed it might be connected with you, Damian,' said PC Nobbs. 'I suspected the boy in the park might be one of your gang.'

'It's a serious offence is dognapping.'

I protested. 'Winston wasn't dognapping. He is one of my trainee detectives and we are saving all the local dogs who are in danger from the Dog Snatcher.'

Mum went pale.

'So where is the dog now?' PC Nobbs asked.

'In the shed,' I explained.

'And Winston?'

'He's gone out to save another dog.'

The policeman headed down the garden towards the shed. He was dead keen to see the dogs. But before he got there, the gate clicked open and Winston walked in. Bad timing! He suddenly found himself face to face with the Law. Was he about to be arrested?

Chapter 8

I couldn't believe what I saw. Winston was standing there with Thumper in one hand and a white poodle in the other.

'You found Blossom!' I yelled. 'Brilliant detective work, Winston. I'll ring Mrs Popperwell.'

I didn't hesitate. I ran back to the house and phoned her straight away. She was thrilled to know her dog was safe and well.

'You are wonderful, Damian,' she said. 'Who else could have found her so quickly? You saved my baby from the Dog Snatcher. I shall come round straight away to get her.'

I would have told Mum the good news but she was in the living room talking to a visitor.

Just as I was about to go out of the back door, she called out, 'Damian! Do you know anything about some posters?'

I didn't say anything.

'Come here, please,' she yelled. 'AT ONCE!'

But I didn't have the time to stop. I had to return to PC Nobbs who had finished questioning Winston and was about to go into the shed.

He should have waited before opening the door. But he didn't.

Thumper and Blossom pushed past him to join the other dogs in the shed, closely followed by the German shepherd so that PC Nobbs was swept along with them.

Our shed is not all that big – several dogs, five kids and a policeman is too much. The dogs were barking and

leaping about and having a great time.
PC Nobbs should have stayed calm,
that's what I say. I don't think he knew
how to handle dogs. He panicked and
that's why he finished up on the floor.

Then Mum arrived with her visitor –

a weird lady called Mrs Peacock. She
wasn't in the least bit interested in our

dog protection work. She kept going on about the misuse of property and said that her posters were blowing all around the town and were ruined. What posters?

But then Mrs Popperwell arrived. Good old Mrs Popperwell. She wouldn't listen to a word Mrs Peacock said, or PC Nobbs. Quite right, too!

'This boy is a genius,' she said. 'You must be so proud of him, Mrs Drooth.'

Mum was looking really mad at me and giving me seriously bad stares. There was going to be trouble later. But Mrs Popperwell didn't take any notice.

'Thank you so much, Damian,' she continued. 'How did you find my dear little Blossom?'

I didn't have time to tell her that Winston had found her. I thought I'd tell her another day.

'I insist that you all come to tea tomorrow,' she continued. 'There will be some important people coming to meet you,' she said. 'I want everyone to know how clever you are.'

Mrs Popperwell left with Blossom. Mrs Peacock left with a few rubbish posters that were lying in the corner of the shed. PC Nobbs left looking very scruffy. I don't think Inspector Crockitt would be pleased to see one of his

officers with his uniform torn and dirty like that.

Soon after, loads of people came to collect the other dogs.

I pointed out that they shouldn't let their dogs loose in the town. All dogs deserve to be safe from Dog Snatchers, that's what I say.

Chapter 9

Mrs Popperwell's party was brilliant. There was loads of food and I especially liked the giant sausage rolls and the chocolate gâteaux. When we had finished eating, she gave a speech.

'Ladies and gentlemen. I would like you to meet the finest detective in town – Damian Drooth. He and his trainee detectives saved my Blossom from the hands of the diabolical Dog Snatcher.'

Everbody cheered (except Mum who was still mad with me for all the damage in the garden).

Inspector Crockitt was at the party, too. It turned out that he was Mrs Popperwell's nephew. After her speech, he took me to one side.

'My aunt seems very pleased with you, Damian. But one of my officers tells me that you've been stealing dogs. I don't like the sound of that.'

I smiled and helped myself to another sausage roll. 'I was working undercover,' I explained.

'Undercover?' Inspector Crockitt replied. 'As what?'

I tapped my nose and winked. 'Top secret,' I said. 'But we got rid of the Dog Snatcher, I think. '

'Who?'

I was surprised his officers hadn't passed on the information.

'Don't worry,' I said. 'He won't dare to come back now he knows we have a crack team of young detectives on the job.'

'What job?'

'Dog protection.'

Inspector Crockitt leaned forward, clenching his teeth. 'You and your detective work,' he growled. 'This time, I'll overlook your behaviour. But watch it, my lad! Just watch it – or you're in serious trouble!' And he walked away.

When I finally got the chance to talk to Winston, I asked him where he had found Blossom. It was quite a surprise.

'She was in our back garden with Thumper,' he said. 'She must have jumped the fence. They really like each other, you know.'

'You mean she escaped the Dog Snatcher?'

'No, Damian. Don't you get it? Blossom wasn't kidnapped. She was in our back garden all the time. There never was a Dog Snatcher.'

I wasn't convinced.

I looked around to see if anyone was listening, then I whispered, 'Don't say a word, Winston. Nobody needs to know how you found her. Keep it to yourself, eh? It's for the best.'

Several weeks later, Blossom surprised everybody by having five puppies that looked like miniature Thumpers. I asked Mum if I could have one of the puppies in the interest of security but she said no. She said she had enough work keeping me under control. I don't understand it, myself. But I shall keep on trying.

NO.1 BOY DETECTIVE

Seek out more mysteries with the No.1 Boy Detective!

Collect them all!